LET'S GET A PET
Harriet Ziefert • Pictures by Mavis Smith

VIKING

In memory of
Sylvia G. Margolin

VIKING
Published by the Penguin Group
Penguin Books USA Inc., 375 Hudson Street, New York, New York 10014, U.S.A.
Penguin Books Ltd, 27 Wrights Lane, London W8 5TZ, England
Penguin Books Australia Ltd, Ringwood, Victoria, Australia
Penguin Books Canada Ltd, 10 Alcorn Avenue, Toronto, Ontario, Canada M4V 3B2
Penguin Books (N.Z.) Ltd, 182–190 Wairau Road, Auckland 10, New Zealand

Penguin Books Ltd, Registered Offices: Harmondsworth, Middlesex, England

First published in 1993 by Viking, a division of Penguin Books USA Inc.

1 3 5 7 9 10 8 6 4 2

Text copyright © Harriet Ziefert, 1993
Illustrations copyright © Mavis Smith, 1993
All rights reserved
Library of Congress Cataloging-in-Publication Data

Ziefert, Harriet.
Let's get a pet/by Harriet Ziefert: illustrated by Mavis Smith.
p. cm.
Summary: Discusses all the things involved in choosing a pet.
ISBN 0-670-84550-7
1. Pets—Juvenile literature. [1. Pets.] I. Smith, Mavis, ill.
II. Title.
SF416.2.Z54 1993
636.088'7—dc20
91-48458 CIP AC

Printed in Singapore for Harriet Ziefert, Inc.

Contents

Which Pet?

One day your parents may say: "You and your sister have been asking for a pet. We've decided this is a good time to get one."

Your sister wants a cat.

You want a dog.

Your parents are not sure they want either a cat or a dog.

Let's get fish.

I'd rather have a bird.

You and your sister argue about which pet is the best.

Cats are boring!

Dogs slobber!

Finally, someone has a good idea.

We need more information. Then we can make a family decision.

Before getting any pet, it's important to ask:

Does the pet need exercise? When and where can we do it?

How much will it cost for supplies and food?

Do we have enough space?

Does anybody have allergies?

Pet Research

You can visit a library.
Different books will tell about different pets.

Talk to people who have pets, or to those who know about them,
like trainers, breeders, and pet store owners.

See for yourself. Observe animals in a pet store...

at an animal shelter...

or at somebody's house.

Making the Right Choice

If you want an animal you can cuddle, then don't get a hedgehog.

If you want a pet you can talk to, then don't get a tarantula.

If you live in a small apartment, then don't get a Great Dane.

If you like a clean sofa, then don't get a Persian cat.

If you want a pet you can teach tricks, then don't get a lizard.

If you want a pet who makes noise, then don't get a rabbit.

If you want a pet who sings a lot, then don't get a female canary.

If you want a pet who's not much trouble, then don't get a puppy.

A Pet Means Commitment

Somebody has to walk the dog.

Somebody has to clean the rabbit hutch.

Somebody has to check the lizard's lamp.

Somebody has to sweep under the bird cage.

Somebody has to clean the turtle bowl.

Somebody has to feed the fish.

Somebody has to buy salt lick for the rabbit.

Somebody has to take Rover to the vet.

Looking at Pets

Small Furry Animals

Mice are nervous animals. It takes a while before they can be handled.
When a mouse gets to know you, it will have fun exploring your pockets.
One mouse is a good pet, but two like to play together and are fun to watch.

Rats are a little bolder than mice and like to play just as much.
If mice and rats are handled often, they lose their fear and
can be taught tricks. They can be taught to:

walk a tightrope

climb a ladder

run a maze

Guinea pigs are not pigs at all. They are friendly little rodents, related to rabbits. Guinea pigs are gentle and timid—easy to hold and fun to watch. They like company, so it's best to keep two together. If you are not interested in breeding guinea pigs, be sure to get two of the same sex.

A rabbit is a quiet, gentle animal. One is best, unless you intend to breed them. When a rabbit gets to know you, it will come to you—even follow you around. A rabbit also likes to sit on a lap and be stroked.

Birds

Birds are pets that can be held and trained. Every bird needs a cage with perches, food, water cups, and playthings, such as a swing and mirror.

A canary is a cheerful pet.
Males sing more than females.

If you are gentle and patient, you can teach a canary to sit on your finger.

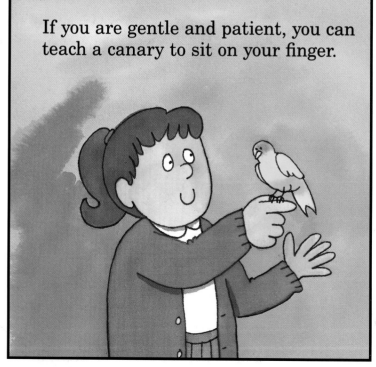

Parrots are expensive. It takes a long time before one will say, "Polly wants a cracker!"

Please, say something.

Parakeets are funny pets. They cock their heads when you talk to them.

If you are patient, you can teach a parakeet to mimic you. But it takes a long time! Remember, a parakeet is imitating the sound of a voice. A talking bird does not understand what it is saying.

19

Fish

Fish are not pets that can be held and petted. But they can be exciting to watch.

Look at the goldfish.

comet nymph

goldfish

fantail

Look at the guppies.

guppy

fantail guppy

A large aquarium can hold many kinds of tropical fish.

angel fish

red swordtail

black mollie

neon tetra

catfish

zebra

Cats

Cats come in different colors, shapes, and sizes.

Cats are curious and playful. Cats play games by themselves and they'll play games with you, too.

When you cuddle a cat, hold it loosely. Stroke it in the direction its fur grows.

Cats purr when they are comfortable.

Dogs

Dogs come in all colors, shapes, and sizes.

You can play games with a dog. Treat a dog with love and care and it will love you in return. A dog can be a real friend and playmate.

You can teach a dog tricks.

A dog will really try to please you.

Making a Decision

Now your parents will probably say, "We've collected information and have been to the pet store. It's time for a family decision."

Your sister still wants a cat.

You still want a dog.

Your sister says, "If we get a cat, I promise to brush my teeth twice a day."

"And I'll make sure the cat uses the scratching post."

You say, "If we get a dog, I promise I'll teach it to obey."

Sit!

TRAIN YOUR DOG

"And I'll walk the dog, too!"

Dad asks, "Do you promise to walk the dog before you go to school?"

"And do you promise to clean the cat's litter box?"

You think about how nice it is to stay in bed.

Your sister thinks about how smelly cat litter can be.

Mom asks, "Do you promise to vacuum after the cat naps?"

"And do you promise to clean up after the dog?"

CURB YOUR DOG

Your sister thinks about how she would rather play than vacuum.

And you think about how yucky dog poop can be.

Dad says, "I think we need to start with something easier to take care of than a kitten, or puppy. How about fish?"

Then Mom says, "Your dad doesn't want a dog. I don't want a cat. You and your sister don't want fish. How about a bird?"

You and your sister have a conference. Together you decide
on something that's not too big, not too small...

not too much trouble...

not too boring...

and not too expensive! Guinea pigs! Two of them!
One for you and one for her!